CU00762103

Praise for *Monkey Magic*

"A beautifully written tale of good vs. evil that will inspire its readers to join the fight to save the orangutan and help save the earth too!"
– JENNI GASKIN, *National Geographic Kids*

"It's a wonderful, magical story. I'm sure children will both benefit from it and love it."
– ZAC GOLDSMITH, environmentalist, politician and writer

"A super book! Please buy it, treasure it in your library and share its message with your family. Then open up the website and text all your friends to follow the instructions so all of you can do your best to help save the orangutans and the rainforests of Borneo in which they live before it is too late."
– DAVID BELLAMY, television presenter, conservationist & writer

"I read *Monkey Magic* to my five-year-old son Robert. He loved this book and is even more inspired to become a Wildlife Warrior!"
– TERRI IRWIN, naturalist and owner of Australia Zoo

"*Monkey Magic* is an enchanting story about a very unusual ape – the orangutan! Living in the steamy rainforests on the remote island of Borneo, orangutans are an extremely endangered species and are encountering many challenges. But a young lady of 11 named Romy suddenly finds herself in the very unique position of being able to help these red apes!"
– "Jungle" Jack Hanna, host of Emmy award-winning *Into the Wild* and Director Emeritus, Columbus Zoo

"A gripping adventure with an important message."
– JEREMY STRONG, bestselling children's author

# About the Author

**Grant S. Clark** has spent much of the past fifteen years writing about primates (the human kind) jumping on each other and chasing balls in his job as a sports journalist. He is British and lives with his family in Singapore.

In this, his first novel, he draws on his experience of spending time in the rainforests of Borneo. Ten percent of the author's royalties will go to conservation charities that help orangutans.

Come and hang out online at www.monkeymagicbook.com.

For free teacher worksheet downloads about conservation, orangutans, *Monkey Magic* and writing, visit the "School Stuff" section at www.monkeymagicbook.com.

Online you can find out what is happening in the world of *Monkey Magic*, post reviews, take quizzes and help save the Orangutan!

# MONKEY MAGIC
## The Curse of Mukada

GRANT S. CLARK

Published by The Can of Worms Kids Press

Published in 2011
by The Can of Worms Kids Press
7 Peacock Yard
Iliffe Street
London
SE17 3LH
www.canofwormsenterprises.co.uk

ISBN: 978-1-904872-37-5

A CIP catalogue record for this book is available from the British
Library

Printed in the UK

**Being friendly to our environment**
We take being friendly to our planet seriously. No animals were
hurt in the making of this book and we have been very careful
with how we use trees. We have only used paper certified by the
Forest Stewardship Council.

**A few more words on recycling**
All the words in Monkey Magic have been recycled. You will
have seen most of them elsewhere but if not please look them
up in a dictionary. Please feel free to send us any words you
might wish to at: info@canofwormsenterprises.co.uk

To Linda, Amy and Rosie

# Contents

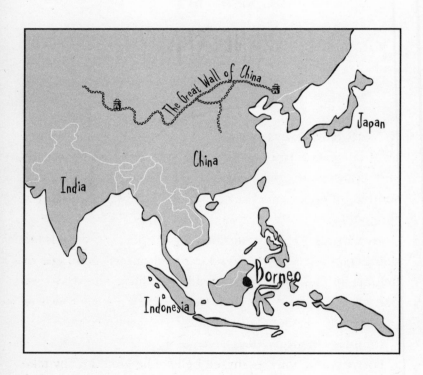

# Chapter 1

# PLANE SCARY

Dad had always promised to take me on one of his faraway journeys, to an exotic land where the smells and tastes were as different to home as the sights and sounds. He's a scientist: an expert on apes and monkeys. A "primatologist", to give it the proper name.

My father, Dr Jeremy Alexander, had spent most of his life doing monkey business. Tracking baboons in the jungle or helping zoo-reared orangutans adjust to life in the wild – all part of a day's work for Dad. He liked to say his job was to protect apes and monkeys from their closest relatives.

He meant humans, of course.

For years, I hadn't let myself believe he would really take me on a trip – mainly to avoid the disappointment in case it never happened. But, deep down, I knew Dad would stick to his word; that's how he was. When I was small, he once bought thirty bags of ice from the petrol station and crushed them with a spade before helping me mould the pieces in the garden. As I stuck a carrot-nose onto the icy face, he said: "There you go, Romy. So what if there's no snow in London again this winter? I promised you'd see a snowman here."

There was as much chance of finding a snowman where we were heading now as there was of spotting a hamster surfing on the moon.

He'd told me a month before the December holidays that the two of us were going to the giant rainforest island of Borneo, in Southeast Asia. If you've heard of Singapore or Bali, Borneo is somewhere between the two and far, far bigger than both put together.

I should know – I spent every night for four weeks before we left scouring maps of Asia.

Dad's task was to work out why orangutans were behaving strangely at the Mukada Nature Reserve. More and more of the ginger-haired apes were migrating to the coast, an area they normally avoided and that was home to proboscis monkeys. The proboscis – famous for their huge rubbery snouts – didn't enjoy orangutans poking their noses around, and the orangutans were falling sick.

We were coming to figure out why.

"Look! The airport," Dad cried, pointing through a window ringed by water droplets. He had to shout to be heard over the whining of the engine in our tiny, rickety plane. I'd held his hand most of the way from the last airport (our third on the journey) and got the feeling from his squeezes that he was almost as frightened as me. My stomach lurched and his grip tightened as the plane suddenly dropped, then jolted upwards.

My other hand clasped the beautiful necklace of blue lapis lazuli beads that Mum had given me as a gift – not for me, unfortunately, but for our hosts. I was happy to wear it for now and clenched it tightly.

As we swooped to our left over the giant rainforest, the airport stood out – excuse the expression – like a monkey's bottom; the grey strip of tarmac was the only break in the blanket of jungle. Lush trees looked like broccoli heads crammed together. We passed a mountain covered in the same green tufts all the way to its peak, the pattern broken

only by a ring of white cloud halfway up.

"Aren't you glad you waited for this trip?" Dad shouted, his smile making his thick brown beard seem even bushier. "Sure beats spending January in Ukraine." I'd complained last year about missing out on his three weeks at a zoo in chilly Ukraine. He was right: this trip was better, and worth waiting for.

"Glad?" I replied. "It's hula time!"

That expression was our family language for fun, for happiness, for excitement. Whenever anyone had reason to be cheerful in the Alexander family, we'd break into a hula. Strapped into my vibrating seat, I couldn't do the wobbly hipped dance, but Dad knew what I meant.

"Well, I'm pleased you came, hula girl."

Of course, he'd never have brought me had he known the danger that lay ahead. But, even looking back later, I wouldn't have changed anything for the world, however perilous the next few days would be. I was about to have the most unforgettable – and scary – time of my first eleven years and seven months of life.

\* \* \*

The plane tilted to the left as the wheels hit the ground with a shudder, making our landing even more terrifying. The pilot grappled with flashing gadgets and a mad joystick. Then suddenly, he was in control: the reverse engines had done their job, and we were slowing on the bumpy, potholed tarmac.

"Phew!" I said, finally releasing Dad's hand. "I was worried then."

"Didn't scare me for one second," he smiled.

"Let's go first class on the way back, though."

If only! The same plane was due to pick us up in a week's time, but I put that to the back of my mind. There was so much to look forward to before then: the beach was supposed to be dreamy, the rainforest dazzling, and, of course, there were the orangutans – my favourite animal for as long as I could remember. For most of my life, I'd fallen asleep cuddling Robbie, my stuffed toy orangutan. Although I had grown out of that, Robbie still sat at the end of my bed.

Was it the orangutans' human-like expressions, their delicate touch, the thirst for fun? Whatever it was, they were the most lovable and fascinating of animals. And to think they might be extinct by the time I got to Dad's age – it filled me with such shame and sadness.

## Chapter 2

# GOLDEN TOOTH

We were the only passengers on the plane, so the green jeep at the end of the runway was almost certainly Dr Nazir, the chief warden of Mukada Nature Reserve. He was due to drive us to our forest lodgings. I was suddenly reminded of my most secret fear for the trip: what would the restrooms be like? I grimaced at the thought of a grimy, insect-infested toilet bowl.

The plane pulled up by a small building with a corrugated iron roof that sat on it like an ill-fitting hat. It was as if we regained our hearing as the roar of the engine gave way to velvety silence.

The man waiting for us was dressed head to toe in brown khakis – the uniform for people in Dad's line of work. Dad had mentioned that the warden had a son about my age called Danny, but there was no sign of anybody else. Our pilot clambered over his seat and grabbed the huge red handle on the plane's door.

"Stomach feeling okay?" he grinned.

"When I get it out of my chest, I'll tell you," Dad replied.

With a sturdy tug, the pilot unlocked the door. It was like opening an oven: the swoosh of air felt like a bucket of warm water. Sweat beads formed on my forehead. Our family holidays in Italy and Spain probably got hotter than this, but the rich dampness seemed to make the air thicker and more stifling.

"Welcome to your first-ever sauna," Dad said, "fully clothed."

"Whoa!" I said, tucking my fleece into a knapsack. "I won't be needing this."

Dad climbed the steps down to the tarmac and turned to help me, just as the man in khakis reached us. Bird cries

and insect calls mingled and echoed to form the music of the forest.

"Dr Alexander, delighted to meet you!" the man said in a squeaky voice followed by a high-pitched laugh. About a foot shorter than Dad, he stretched a hand up to reach my father's. "I'm Dr Nazir."

He laughed again, revealing a golden tooth.

"Good to meet you, too. But please call me Jeremy. And this is my daughter, Romy."

They shook hands, and Dr Nazir peered at me.

"How was the journey, my dear?"

He laughed his strange laugh again. I was usually shy meeting new people – especially slightly weird ones – but the excitement pushed those feelings aside.

"Great, thanks! I was so scared when the plane – "

"Very good," he interrupted and laughed again, looking back to my father. "Let's get going now. No time to gossip as it'll be dark soon."

"Suits us," said Dad, his brown sleeves folded to the elbows and a Panama hat shading his squinting eyes. "We've got work to do," Dad continued, striding in khaki trousers almost twice as long as the warden's.

"I fear that your journey may be wasted," said Dr Nazir. "I can tell you straight away what the problem is. I said to the governor there's no need to spend money flying a so-called expert in when it's as clear as daylight what's going on with the orang – ."

It was my father's turn to interrupt rudely.

"I thought we were in a hurry, Dr Nazir?"

Dad often arrived on a job only to hear that his presence wasn't appreciated. Dr Nazir squealed another high-pitched laugh, but his eyes looked serious.

"Silly me," he said. "I get so lonely out here, and I do like to chat. You will see, though."

We climbed into the jeep just as the melting sun dribbled over the top of the towering trees. The sun's exit didn't seem to affect the temperature, and I used a giant leaf to the top of the towering trees. The sun's exit didn't seem to affect the temperature, and I used a giant leaf to fan my face.

"We don't have far to go," said Dr Nazir. "I do hope you brought mosquito repellent."

He giggled his bizarre laugh again, his tooth reflecting gold sparkles onto the jeep's dashboard.

* * *

Darkness was approaching when we reached the base, but there was enough light to make out the golden-sanded beach, a short stroll from where we parked. It was straight out of a holiday brochure, with palm trees lining the crescent-shaped bay and clear blue water lapping the shore. The tide was heading out, leaving a sprinkling of jewel-like shells and blobby masses of jellyfish carcasses. The sun had slurred a deep orange and purple trail to the horizon.

I ran straight from the jeep for a paddle. Being used to the sea off the coast of England, I braced myself for the chill. Instead, it was like a warm bath. I leant to pick up a shell and almost jumped when it started running. I noticed dozens, no hundreds, of shells doing the same. I grabbed a bright red one shaped like a snail. A collection of scrawny legs poked out and performed some air-running before disappearing.

"A hermit crab," said Dad, catching up with me. "Come on, honey, you'll have plenty of time for the beach. We need to unpack."

I lowered the crab carefully by the edge of the water, unsure whether it had been heading for land or sea. Did it have a plan, I wondered, or was it running around without a purpose, hoping for everything to become clear?

I stared at the coast as might someone arriving on a boat after a long journey: palm trees lined up like soldiers protecting the shore. Beyond the trees was a grassy clearing about the size of a football field. Walking around as if it owned the place was a huge pot-bellied pig, chomping away with its head buried. A row of wooden buildings that had seen better days lined the field. A giant desk on a woodbeamed platform sat at the front of the middle building, with broken seats scattered around.

The guest chalets were on either side, each perched on stilts with wooden steps leading to a balcony. Dad was hauling our rucksacks up to one of the chalets. He stopped to wipe his brow and wave.

I ran to help but stopped dead still: someone was sitting on the low branch of a tree next to me. It was a boy, about my age. He had dark hair and wore nothing but a pair of long, cream shorts, frayed below the knee. I guessed it was Danny. I walked on, turned around and saw him staring into the forest, seeming not to notice me. His eyes were brown and piercing, even in the fading light of dusk. I lifted my hand to wave, stopped myself and instead scratched my shoulder.

I walked on and climbed the creaky steps to our hut. The room was – to be generous – basic. The sheets on the two rusty metal beds were clean at least, but the stained pillows looked like they'd been shared by an army. Thankfully the windows had mosquito screens. A sign nailed to the wall was written in different languages including English: Beware! Thieves! Lock your windows at all times

Underneath was a picture of a monkey.

"That's serious, by the way," Dad remarked. "I've lost several cameras and goodness-knows-how-much laundry to monkey thieves!"

"So that's why those gibbons were wearing your socks in Indonesia!"

"Actually it was my boxer shorts."

I'm no prissy princess, but this was no place you'd take someone you were trying to impress – unless they had spent the past few years living on a rubbish tip. The smell was part damp, part toilet.

"Don't worry," Dad said, reading my thoughts. "You've got the luxury room next door, unless you're a bit nervous and want to share?"

"I'll be fine on my own," I said, not totally convinced.

I opened a squeaky door and entered our shared restroom for the moment of truth. The shower was a grubby hosepipe hooked to the wall with coat-hanger wire, but – hoorah! – the toilet looked clean and even had spare paper. Mosquitoes perched on the ceiling, waiting to strike. I was virtually lacquered with repellent so I didn't interest them for now.

The other door in the restroom opened onto my room.

It was an exact replica of Dad's, right down to the monkey sign and dirty pillows.

"This isn't the worst room I've seen," said Dad, smiling as he sat on one of the beds in my room. "The one through there is just as bad."

We burst out laughing. He had warned me not to expect luxury, and once again he had been true to his word.

# Chapter 3

# THE BOY FROM THE TREE

After aiming the dribble of tepid water from the hosepipe over my head for ten minutes, I finally felt like I had cleaned away the grime from our twenty-four hour journey. Dad was reading on his bed when I walked in. There was a knock at the door, and a giggle followed.

"Jeremy? Romy? Are you ready for dinner?"

"Just coming, Dr Nazir," Dad said, looking at me and raising his eyebrows.

I opened the door, and we were smothered by the glow of a bonfire, dancing in the middle of the grass clearing. A tall man wearing – guess what – khakis was prodding something in the fire. The pig was still head down munching away, its plump body orange in the firelight.

"Follow me, dear guests," the doctor said, his golden tooth glistening.

The exhausting journey might have taken an entire day,

but the amazingly clear night sky, peppered with brilliant stars, was doing its best to talk me out of feeling tired. We followed the warden and sat on a rug just beyond spitting range of the embers. The other man, much younger than the doctor, smiled.

"This is Anton, my deputy," Dr Nazir declared.

"Is this the most beautiful girl in Borneo?" Anton said in some sort of European accent, laughing loudly. "And is that the bushiest beard in the tropics? Pleasure to meet you both."

Anton shook Dad's hand, then leant on his knee and took my hand and planted a kiss. He was as tall as Dad, and his spiky blond hair made him seem even bigger.

"Princess Romy. It is an honour! And tell me this: do you know why the monkeys stopped playing football in the jungle?"

"Huh?" I replied.

"Because there were too many cheetahs!"

He burst into hysterics and prodded me jokingly. Anton seemed much more fun than Dr Nazir, and I couldn't stop myself laughing as he ran around the fire doing an impression of a baboon.

"Anton knows the reserve inside out, much better than me," Dr Nazir said. "Even if he is a bit crazy."

"This is a place of dreams," Anton said, looking serious now and gazing into the night. "The stars, the forest, the animals. Welcome to heaven on Earth."

"It is breathtaking," Dad said. "Will Danny be joining us, doctor? Romy was looking forward to making a friend."

There was a pause.

"He's not here, I'm afraid, but he may be later." Dr Nazir stared into the distance.

"I think I saw him earlier," I said.

"I don't think so," he snapped.

Sorry I spoke!

Anton used tongs to pull a pan from the flames and poured a rich-smelling sauce onto our rice-covered plates.

"Vegetable curry," he declared proudly. "Not so spicy, for your sensitive British mouths!"

Eggplant, potatoes and beans swam in a sumptuous yellow liquid that tasted even yummier when absorbed by the sticky rice. We munched away and had second helpings before Anton peeled a green-skinned fruit the size of a coconut and cut me a slice. I took it straight from the penknife, and the sweetness fizzed in my mouth.

"The mangoes here are the best," he said. "Just ask the monkeys."

"So what about the orangutans then?" Dad said, turning to Dr Nazir. "What is this obvious reason you mentioned before why the orangutans are heading to the coast?"

"It's simple," Dr Nazir reflected. "Overpopulation."

Dad half coughed, half choked.

"Surely not?" he sputtered. "Their numbers are dwindling everywhere."

"Not here. We're a victim of our own success. We have created a breeding ground for all species, and they are flourishing, especially the apes and monkeys, and particularly the orangutans."

"Have you got the numbers?"

"Who needs numbers? Just open your eyes. Orangutans have never had it so good, and now they are getting restless and looking for new ground. The only thing keeping them here is the sea. It's true, isn't it Anton?"

"I know it sounds ludicrous," said Anton. "But it's probably right. I have been here for five years, and we've never had so many Os. It's strange to say, but it's got to the stage where there are too many. There isn't enough food, and they cannot always find fresh water."

"That's why they get sick?" Dad asked.

"That's Anton's conclusion," explained the warden. "I mean, our conclusion."

"Well that's something you don't hear often," Dad said. "Why don't you move them to the other reserves, where there's space?"

"It's a good idea," Anton said. "That's exactly what we proposed."

"But they sent you instead," said the doctor.

That wasn't so friendly.

"Overpopulation would certainly be unusual," said Dad. "There were hundreds of thousands of orangutans not so long ago. Now there are just fifty thousand or so, maybe fewer. Too many just isn't a problem."

"It is here, my friend," said Dr Nazir. "It is here."

* * *

"Night, darling," said Dad, kissing me on the forehead. "Big day tomorrow."

"Sleep well, Dad," I replied, yawning.

He closed the door to our shared bathroom, leaving me with a torch gripped to my chest. Outside, I could hear the jungle noises. Night-time is the loudest time in the rainforest, when insects go crazy and all sorts of creatures scream themselves silly. I was a terrible sleeper at the best of times and had spent countless hours lying in bed with my mind racing. Sleeping was going to be a real challenge here.

I was just beginning to relax when a loud crack came from the front of our chalet, followed by a bump. I thought I heard someone say "Ouch!". I jumped out of bed, opened the curtain and looked out at the moonlit view. Something was moving in the bushy trees across the clearing. I squinted and could make out a child sitting at the bottom of one of the trees where I'd spotted the boy earlier. He looked as though he had fallen off or a branch had snapped. I opened my door and climbed carefully down the steps.

"Are you okay?" I said in a loud whisper.

No response. I walked closer and repeated the question, now just fifteen or so paces away. Was it the same boy I'd seen earlier, the one in the tree? He turned, and I met his piercing eyes.

"Thank you for ask," he said in an accent much stronger than Dr Nazir's. "Sore bum!"

It was indeed the boy in the frayed shorts. He got up and smiled, revealing goofy teeth that were almost fluorescent in the moonlight.

"You who?" he asked.

"I beg your pardon?"

"You who?"

"Oh. My name's Romy. And you must be Danny?"

"Call me Danny if like."

"Hi, Danny. Nice to meet you."

"You see sky?"

I peered up. Then I jumped as I felt a tickle under my chin. Looking down, I saw a pink flower dabbing my neck. It was on the end of a long stick Danny was holding.

"Tickle funny!" he laughed. "No mean to scare, sorry."

I smiled back and took the flower from the stick.

Danny strolled to the fire, sat down and stared into the orangey-red heat. He looked back and waved for me to join him. I didn't know what to do but found myself tiptoeing over. His silky skin was the colour of milky coffee, but his feet were rough and marked. I noticed a scar stretching over the top of his left foot, like a twisting snake.

Sitting down no more than an arm's length away, I gazed into the dying embers with him. No one spoke for minutes, but, strangely enough, it didn't feel awkward. How is it that some people you've only just met seem like old friends, while others leave you cold?

He broke the silence, his eyes fixed on the fire.

"This is mystical place. Families living here centuries and passing power, mother to child."

"It's a very special place," I said, marvelling at a giant palm tree silhouetted by the moon.

"You here like others? To take? Or to give?"

"Dad and I are here to help the orangutans."

"They always say same," he said. "But I sense different. I see good among evil. You friend."

"I love orangutans," I whispered.

"Orangutans love humans for years. But now different. You know story of Curse of Mukada?"

"Curse of what?"

"Mukada was village many years ago. Terrible fire. People trapped as fire burned, children cry, mothers scream. Death about to visit. Then from sky comes hand of orangutan."

He sprang to his feet in a crouching position, with his arms stretched.

"And then more furry hands come down," he continued with his arms waving, his eyes bright, his voice excited. "Children pulled first into trees, then mothers, then fathers. All to safety. The night sky turned to red from fire. Orangutans save whole village, except for boy."

"A boy? What happened to him?"

"Nobody knowing, but they say flames took him to next world."

He sat down again.

"Parents never forgive ape for saving brother but leaving him. Family wanted orangutan to suffer as they suffer. They start curse. Orangutans dying ever since. Curse continues unless death is repaid at Mukada and sky turns blood red."

"Death repaid? The sky turns blood red?"

"That is curse."

"That's so sad, especially as the orangutans saved so many lives."

"We humans strange and cruel."

"But people are also good. Surely the curse can be stopped. I mean, if you believe it?"

"Curse real." A door banged, and I turned to see Dad

standing outside our hut, pointing a torch.

"Are you all right, Romy?" he cried. "What are you doing?"

"I'm fine, Dad. Come and meet Danny."

"Danny?" muttered Dad.

I turned back to see an empty space, but for the pink flower where Danny had sat. There was a shuffle of leaves behind me and another rustle above my head, but Danny had gone. What a mysterious boy!

"You must have scared him away," I said, back at the bungalow. "I guess we'll see him tomorrow."

"Go to bed, darling. You need some sleep."

One of the cool things about the equator is that the sun rises at roughly 7 am and sets at about 7 pm – twelve hours of day and night each day. Very predictable. I was starting to feel sleepy from the travel, even though it was mid-afternoon back home. It felt like the middle of the night here, yet it was still only 9 pm.

There was plenty of time for sleep, plenty of time for monkey magic.

## Chapter 4

# GIVE ME A BANANA

Even the cicadas drumming their legs outside couldn't compete with the sound blasting through the wall. Mum had always complained about Dad's snoring, and now I could hear why.

Knowing he was asleep made me feel uneasy, like I was alone. I thought about moving to the spare bed in his room. The racket he was making convinced me to stay put though, and I pointed the torchlight at the ceiling. Mosquitoes sat patiently, waiting for me to doze off. I'd smothered myself in repellent again to try to disappoint them. I switched the light off, and the gleaming circle of the moon filtered through the curtain.

Closing my eyes, I thought about Danny's story – the heroic orangutans, the poor child left behind, the wretched curse of Mukada – but sleep finally interrupted, as if a dark cloak had smothered my thoughts.

* * *

The drumming started faintly. It grew louder and louder, maintaining the same 1-2-3, 1-2-3, 1-2-3 tempo.

Then I noticed the chanting.

I looked down and realized I was at the top of a tree!

Grabbing a branch, I swung to the next tree. The air felt soothing and the leaves brushed my hair like limp fingers. I moved nervously at first but soon gained confidence. The chanting and drumming were loud enough that they couldn't be coming from too far away. I kept swinging and reached the top of a tree that towered above the others. From there, I noticed a break in the forest, an area with no treetops about the size of a tennis court.

Orange light flickered around the tops of the trees at the edge. There must be a clearing. I moved more urgently and stubbed my toe on a thick branch but kept going, desperate to get to the source of the music. Maybe it wasn't humans. It was more of a grunting sound than voices.

Then the tempo changed, suddenly, as did the voices. "Ooh, ooh, give me a banana," the chant went. "Ooh, ooh, give me a banana."

I laughed and wondered who was singing this silly verse. There couldn't be more than ten trees to go, and I clasped a bendy branch with my left hand, then grabbed another with my right as I swept along at full speed. Nearly there.

The chanting was now almost deafening, and the

drumming reverberated through my head like drilling.

"Ooh, ooh, give me a banana – ooh, ooh, give me a banana."

The orange glow was from a fire. I could see the tops of the flames as I got to the last tree before the clearing and strained to look into the cauldron from which the sound echoed.

There was a tap on my shoulder.

I didn't want to open my eyes, but the tapping was firm and insistent.

My left eyelid felt like it had weights attached to it, but I forced it open and nearly jumped out of bed.

I was no longer dreaming, or was I? With both eyes now wide, I glared at the creature cowering nervously in the corner of my room, the creature that had tapped my shoulder.

Its orange hair was thick, its eyes gentle, its hands human-like. I wanted to scream but couldn't, partly because it looked more scared than me, partly out of curiosity.

The orangutan then spoke. Yes, really. It spoke.

"Need help," it said.

"W-w-what?" My voice trembled.

"Shush! No wake father man." The orangutan slowly opened the window and looked back at me. It was as tall as me, with muscular arms twice as long as its body. The moonlight reflected against shiny, orange-brown hair hanging from its limbs.

"Come, fast. Bring medicine."

What could I do? Surely this was still a dream, so I went along with it, as you do in dreams. I picked up my knapsack and stuffed in the medical kit Mum had packed. I also threw in two bottles of water and a few bananas from a fruit bowl.

"W-w-where are we going?"

"You see already, no? You hear the chants?"

"That was a dream."

"My children sick. By way, me Larnie."

"Sorry?"

"I called Larnie. I mother of Nina and Didi."

Introducing yourself to an ape isn't as easy as you'd think. Do you shake hands, kiss on the cheek or start grooming each other's hair?

"Oh, hello, Larnie. I'm Romy."

"Follow me. And watch!"

The orangutan jumped from the window and grabbed at a branch. I'd no idea why, but it felt completely natural to do the same, and I sprang from the window without fear. I caught hold of a branch with my right arm and seized another with my left. Soon we were near the top of the canopy and heading into the deep of the forest, guided by the moonlight. Larnie looked over her shoulder, and I was sure she actually winked!

We kept going for ten minutes, and I was starting to feel a little heavy-armed when we came to where the river met the sea. A man stood staring out at the ocean.

Hang on: it was Dr Nazir. What could he be doing?

The orangutan didn't stop and followed the river inland for a few minutes, then, when I finally caught up, put her finger over her mouth as if to tell me to keep quiet. Even with the bustling noise of the night-time jungle, it was easy to make out the low hum of an engine. And in the moonlight, a long barge could be clearly seen on the river. Its cargo was covered by a giant green canvas bearing a palm tree logo and the letter M.

"What is that?" I asked, but the orangutan had already set off, so I followed. After another ten minutes, the rainforest came to an abrupt end, and there was a giant clearing way below us. Again, Larnie signalled for silence, and we remained still, just as a puff of smoke wafted up. Was there a fire, I wondered? No, there were voices, and then I recognized the smell: cigarettes. Groups of men trudged from the forest dragging massive branches. There were at least fifty, maybe a hundred men. The branches were covered in green leaves, so must have been freshly cut. They seemed to be spreading the branches evenly around the clearing then going back for more. Others were digging holes.

What on earth were they doing?

Larnie was to my left, and I jumped as something tapped my right shoulder twice. I quickly looked around to see what was there but noticed the ape withdrawing her giant arm behind me.

"Sorry," Larnie whispered, giggling. "We love that trick. Come on, let's go."

Before I had time to respond, my orangutan guide was gliding though the trees. I took another look at the men below, carrying out their strange business in the middle of the night, then set off again. Within minutes I thought I heard some drumming. Yes, there was a chant, too. And the light was coming from a clearing ahead of us. It was just like the dream. It probably still was a dream. It had to be, surely? How else could I be hurtling through the trees like a monkey and chatting with an orangutan called Larnie? But it seemed so real.

"Ooh, ooh, give me a banana," came the chant. I reached the top of the canopy and looked down to see four orangutans, perched about halfway up the trees on a platform of branches, twigs and leaves, chanting their funny song. Larnie climbed down and joined the others.

"Quick," she beckoned.

I jumped the last few metres, expecting to hurt my legs, but felt no pain. The apes all stared at me, including two babies which were lying down.

What did you do in this situation? I knew how to act at a friend's house or when visiting a relative, but nothing had prepared me for a trip to an orangutan family. I pulled the knapsack off my back and held out the bananas.

It was as if I had just told the best joke in the world.

The three adult orangutans burst into hysterics and jumped

on each other playfully. The biggest climbed a tree in five seconds and then came down as quickly. From nowhere, a foot snatched the bananas.

"Thank you kindly," the big orangutan said, his eyes almost level with mine, even though he was sitting down with the bananas between his toes. "I am Dunga."

"You were asking for bananas," I said sheepishly. "I mean in the song."

Again they burst out laughing. "We do like a banana," said Dunga, pulling one with his hand from the bunch that he gripped with his feet.

"But we do singing to cheer up my children Nina and Didi. They sick, and that is favourite song."

The adults pointed at the baby orangutans. The cute apes had little energy but seemed to smile back at me. Thin, wispy

hair stuck out of their brown skin as if they had suffered an electric shock. Circles of pink skin surrounded their cheeky, oval brown eyes, the same pink colour as their mouths and snouts. They were adorable!

"You funnily looking," said one baby in a squeaky voice. "Your hair banana colour!" The other baby laughed softly and then grimaced in pain.

"What is wrong with them?" I asked.

"We don't know, but we think maybe bad water," said Larnie, who was only half the size of Dunga and far prettier. "We move from heart of forest and now water tasting bad."

Maybe it's seawater, I thought. The orangutans were shifting to the coast; that's why Dad was here. Perhaps it was harder to find fresh water. Salt water caused dehydration, and the young are more likely to suffer from a lack of water, as Mum had lectured me for years.

"Try this," I said, opening the bottles of water.

Dunga swiped them from my hand and held them to the infants' mouths. They gulped the water down and swallowed the bananas practically whole.

There was a double-tap on my right shoulder, and I looked around to see nothing. The apes burst into laughter again as I fell for the same trick as before, this time from the hand of the other adult, a much older orangutan.

To show them how much fun I was having, I got up and started doing the hula. The young orangutans rolled on their backs, laughing. Suddenly, three adult orangutans were trying to do the hula with me. We all giggled, and I stuck my left arm around the old orangutan's back. I tapped its left shoulder, and it jerked its head, startled. The rest fell onto their backs in hysterics.

When the laughter died down, Dunga held up his hand for silence.

"See the moon," he said, pointing just above the treetops (don't ask how I knew Dunga was a "he").

"Monkey magic only works in moonlight and when you sleeping. You must return soon."

"Monkey magic?" I asked.

"It's why you here," said Dunga, his face framed by leathery, brown pads – a feature of grown-up males. "It's how you here. Monkey magic only works on the one who can save us."

"I will take her, Dunga," said Larnie, turning to me.

"You will come back tomorrow? That okay, Shalan?"

"Yes, she is the one." The older orangutan, with grey hair in his ginger coating, turned to me. "You can stop the dying."

"What can I do?" I asked.

"What you see tonight," Larnie said. "The humans dragging the forest, the man by the sea, the boat. What does it mean? We cannot know."

"And remember this, human friend," Shalan said. "Follow the Cyclops."

Follow the Cyclops! This was getting stranger by the minute.

"If I see one I will follow it," I said.

"You must go now."

"It was a pleasure meeting you," I said, facing them all on the nest that they would probably discard the next day for a new one. Orangutans rarely stay in the same place from one night to the next.

Nina and Didi sat up for the first time and stared at me wide-eyed.

"Thanks for help," said Dunga, holding out a green object. It was a mango! "This for you."

I put it in my knapsack and headed off into the trees with Larnie. We were soon at the chalet, just as the moon reached the horizon. I climbed through the window, and Larnie perched on the frame. She held out her giant arm and delicately squeezed my hand.

In an instant she was gone.

## Chapter 5

# THE MAN ON THE TREETOPS

"Hey sleepyhead, wake up," Dad whispered. "How come your window's open?"

I opened my eyes slowly, recalling the amazing dream. Or was it a dream? The window was open – I was sure it had been locked last night.

I wanted to tell him about the dream, but it was so strange I didn't know where to start. I also wanted to see Danny again. He wouldn't laugh if I told him what had happened. He might even be able to explain the dream. He had said the rainforest had mystical power.

"Morning, Dad," I yawned. "Boy, you can snore."

"You sound like your Mum."

"You sound like a rhino."

I was thirsty and reached for one of the bottles of water. They were gone. I put my hand in my knapsack and felt something cool and smooth. I pulled out a mango! So it really had happened! How could I explain to Dad?

I decided to wait before saying anything. There was so much to take in. The boat on the river and Dr Nazir, the men in the forest, the wonderful, friendly orangutans, my new friend Danny, my transformation into a tree-swinger!

I would have plenty of time to think it through today. We were going on a helicopter trip over the reserve in the morning and then trekking to a forest lodge in the afternoon to stay for one night. Maybe the pillows wouldn't be so grimy there. I had thrown mine off the bed last night because of the smell. Now Dad picked it up from the wood-beamed floor.

"And I thought you were too old for imaginary friends," Dad said, smiling.

"What do you mean?"

"The extraordinary vanishing Danny!"

"He was real! You'll see him today."

"I'm just pulling your leg. Of course he's real. Dr Nazir has only one son. And talking of the strange Dr Nazir, he has gone down with a tummy bug so won't be taking us on the tour today. Quite a relief, actually, as Anton seems much more clued up."

"He doesn't seem to resent us being here, unlike the doctor," I said.

"I know what you mean," Dad said. "Hey, your legs are covered in muck! You had better take another hosepipe."

"Hosepipe?"

"Well you can hardly call it a shower. And look at your

toe! How did you bruise it so badly?"

\* \* \*

"There's no better way for a princess with golden hair and eyes like opals to view the reserve than by helicopter," Anton declared, bowing before me. I giggled, mostly out of embarrassment.

"Climb aboard, dear Romy. I hope you can steer this thing!"

"I hope you are joking," said Dad, getting in beside me.

"I learnt how to fly a helicopter in Serbia years ago," said Anton. "I wasn't always a park ranger."

"So that's the accent!" Dad said. "I didn't think you were from this neck of the forest."

"No, but it's home now," Anton said, flicking switches on the dashboard. "I've outstayed one chief warden here, and I'll probably outlast a second one."

"What do you mean?" Dad inquired.

"Dr Nazir is – how do you say – rather distracted, and I fear is going the same way as the previous warden. The man who preceded Dr Nazir actually went nuts and disappeared into the forest a couple of years ago. We occasionally see him running around wild. He's past help."

"So what's wrong with the doctor?" Dad asked. "Why is he distracted?"

"He has some personal issues, and he just seems to have

given up caring. In this business, if you stop caring about the animals, you stop caring about life. He actually pleaded with me not to take you over the reserve; he wanted us to just stick to the coast today."

"Why would he want that?" Dad asked.

"Who knows?"

The blades started to rotate, and Anton shouted: "We may have to make it a short trip today because the winds are up. Put your helmets on."

With that, the engine roared and we climbed into the sky rather more smoothly than our plane had the day before.

"We are going very high," Dad shouted to Anton through the microphones on our helmets. My ears were popping.

"It's to avoid the winds above the forest."

"What winds?" Dad asked, but got no answer.

I knew what he meant. It was a calm, still day, and the tops of the towering trees barely swayed in the gentle breeze. It hardly made sense for Anton to take us so high.

We headed inland and went so high that it was hard to make out much other than the green and yellow blanket of treetops. I stared down and was startled by something tiny, though: at the top of the forest canopy, a person, a man, I think, was standing with his arms outstretched in the air. I lost him briefly but looked back down and saw him again. There was something huge on his back – maybe a bag or a sack.

"Dad, look!" I cried, but at that instant the man jumped

from the top of the trees and dived into the jungle! How had he climbed up there? And was he all right? That was a long way to fall. "What is it, Romy?"

"It was a man. I'm sure. On top of the ..."

"A man?" Dad asked.

"I'm pretty sure it was," I said, wondering if I'd really seen what I thought I had. After the night before, I wasn't sure about anything.

"Are you seeing things?" Anton smiled. "Let me know if you see a mountain of gold!"

Again, I wanted to tell Dad everything, but it all appeared so bizarre. How could a man jump from the top of the forest?

"Can we go lower?" Dad asked Anton.

The helicopter suddenly thrust to the left, and I grabbed Dad's knee to steady myself. I was looking straight down to the ground through the glass side of the chopper and felt a rush of fear. It was even more frightening than the plane. Another jolt, to the right this time, took my breath away.

"It's no good," Anton declared. "The winds. We've got to return. At least you have seen where the orangutans lived before migrating."

"Strange winds these," Dad replied.

* * *

We set off with Anton after lunch for the forest lodge,

heading along the path that followed the coast. Grey rhesus monkeys eyed us with suspicion, some brave enough to run up and scream. I was a little frightened when they grabbed at my knapsack, but Anton shooed them away.

"Never look them in the eye," he warned. "That's when they'll attack."

We reached the river mouth, where the tide was out, leaving a swampy landscape of mangrove trees.

Dad spotted the first one.

"Look. Over the bridge!"

There, in the distance, was the strange sight of five proboscis monkeys jogging across the mud, their arms dangling by their feet. They stopped at a mangrove tree and climbed up to devour its leaves. We walked cautiously over and watched for five minutes as their huge rubber noses,

drooping over their mouths, wobbled with every bite. Anton pointed towards the sea at several groups of proboscis monkeys, with their comical faces and large bellies.

One of them jumped several metres from one tree to the next, surprisingly agile for something so bulky. The leap reminded me of my adventure the previous night. Dad had told me before that their stomachs were so big because they have a complicated way of digesting food, and that copying their diet in captivity was almost impossible. That's why you rarely see a proboscis monkey at a zoo.

He had also told me that the bigger-nosed monkeys were the males. The locals nicknamed them "Dutch monkey" because their tummies and snouts reminded them of people from the Netherlands who used to live in their country. Not very flattering.

"You can only see these guys in Borneo now," whispered Anton. "That's another reason we don't want the orangutans snooping around on their patch. These monkeys are endangered, too, and there are even fewer of them than there are Os."

So where were all these orangutans? I wondered. I could tell Dad was thinking the same thing as he scanned the scene, seeming not to notice the proboscis monkeys. Anton led us along a wooden platform directly into the rainforest and we turned down a path that followed the curve of the coast.

Across the mucky low-tide terrain, in the distance, I

spotted some movement. The path took us towards the sea but via some thick vegetation that shielded us from the beach. Then we turned a corner and there they were before us: 100, maybe even 150 orangutans.

"Blow me down sideways!" exclaimed Dad.

"Unbelievable," I said.

"No shortage of orangutans here," smiled Anton.

"I've never seen so many together," said Dad. "Extraordinary."

"We just need to herd some inland and ship the rest to another reserve and the problem is solved," declared Anton. "Nazir may be going nuts, but he is right when it comes to these creatures."

"But why would they come here unless ..." Dad paused, "... unless they had to?"

"All due respect, but they aren't as clever as you scientists presume," Anton said. "You can see how many there are: this reserve is simply producing too many orangutans."

"There's no such thing as too many," I said.

"Well, true," said Anton. "But there are too many for this reserve."

"Anton, that area we flew over today, by my estimate, is a couple of miles inland, right?" asked Dad.

"Yes, maybe more. You saw the conditions were perfect."

Dad did not say anything.

We stayed for a while, investigating the scene on the beach. While Dad took hundreds of photos, I looked out for my orangutan friends but couldn't spot Shalan, Dunga or Larnie, let alone Nina or Didi. I was worried about the two infants; I prayed they were getting better and couldn't wait to go to sleep tonight, so I might see them again.

Would the monkey magic repeat itself?

The lodge was another thirty minutes away, along a jungle path covered with finger-like tree roots, pools of blood-red water and plants with spikes that could rip your flesh. Although the water was coloured red by leaves and bark, not by blood, I trod very carefully to make sure I didn't add to the effect.

\* \* \*

The lodge was split into two rooms, as basic as the ones at the base. I shared with Dad this time, while Anton took the other room. We were all tired out by the time he served up another delicious, steaming concoction from a billycan.

"So what do you think, Dr Alexander?" said Anton, sitting on the balcony overgrown with branches and clinging plants.

"You could well be right about the overpopulation," Dad said. "I've yet to see anything that proves you wrong."

I knew the way Dad usually spoke – and that was a funny thing for him to say.

I desperately wanted to tell them about the boat and the men dragging branches and everything else. I thought they might have something to do with the extraordinary number of orangutans we had seen today. But how would I explain it? I'd wait until we were in our room because I didn't want to recount my ridiculous story in front of Anton.

Still, I thought I'd drop something into the conversation.

"I'm sure I saw some barges on the river," I said matter-of-factly. "I wonder what they were doing."

"When did you see that?" asked Anton sharply.

"Maybe when we flew in?" I lied.

There was a pause before Anton spoke. "There's a rubber plantation way up river. It must have been from there."

"Is there something wrong with the trees we flew over this morning?" Dad then asked. "They seem to be yellowing in sections."

"No, that's the usual cycle for many of our species," Anton explained. "Even leaves in the rainforest eventually die."

"But that's not – " Dad stopped. "It doesn't matter."

I had noticed a path near the front of the lodge, heading off the main track into the forest. Now I asked Anton about it.

"Probably best to avoid it, since it's sacred for the few villagers left in the forest," he said.

"Where does it lead?" I inquired.

Anton chuckled. "To hell, according to the locals. They say it is where a boy's ghost wanders: a boy who died in a fire at Mukada village years ago. But as far as I know, it just takes you into the darkest part of the forest. Either way, it's not really worth the risk."

\* \* \*

Dad switched off the light and got into his bed.

"Something's not right," he said, yawning. "I've never seen so many yellow trees in a rainforest. And what was all that about winds above the forest when it seemed calm?"

"Actually, some strange things have been happening," I whispered, relieved I could at last talk to Dad alone.

"Like what?"

Anton began clonking around in the next room and coughed; the walls of the lodge were like paper, and if we could hear him, I thought he could probably hear everything we said, so I waited a few minutes for silence.

"I don't really know how to explain," I began, in a whisper. "It started with a weird dream. I was swinging through the jungle like a monkey and heard this chanting and then – "

The sound of snoring stopped me.

"Dad?"

He was already fast asleep. Oh, Dad! It would have to wait until morning.

I was dying to fall asleep, hoping for more monkey magic so I could discover whether Didi and Nina were better. I had brought extra water and fruit just in case. They were already packed in my knapsack. Lying with my eyes closed, I desperately tried to doze off but could not. Eventually I started thinking of nothing but the colour black. It was a trick a doctor had once told me to try, a way of helping me fall asleep when my mind was racing. Shiny shapes floated in the blackness, and I was soon relaxing.

Then came a tap at my shoulder. "Come," a voice said.

I opened my eyes and saw Larnie.

"It's Nina and Didi. Quick!" she said.

* * *

I followed her out of the window into the moonlit night. We soon reached the others on a new nest in the trees. Nina and Didi lay still on Dunga's lap.

I passed the water.

"Are they okay?" I asked worriedly.

There was silence. Suddenly, the two infants got up and jumped on top of me, tickling my chin. Everyone laughed.

"Thanks to you, they are getting better," said Dunga. "Water is best medicine."

I was overcome with relief. Thank goodness they were OK. I smiled as the two infants climbed all over me, at one time both hanging on to my head! They instinctively seemed to know that my most ticklish spot was under the arms. They buried themselves into my sides as I tried to lock my arms against my body and stop their attack.

I managed to grip Nina under one arm and Didi under the other, and Dunga started tickling their feet with his toes, causing the squeakiest laughs I had ever heard. I released them, and they only stopped prodding me when Larnie and

Shalan tried doing the hula. Nina and Didi joined in, while swigging water. Nina then jumped on my shoulder and began stroking my hair with fingers no bigger than caterpillars.

"Why you not hairier?" said Nina. "You look funny."

"Funny arms, too," said Didi, giggling and holding my hand. "So small. No good for swinging!"

Nina climbed down my back and grabbed my bottom. "Why you cover up botty?" Nina laughed at my trousers. "You not do poo-poo?"

All the apes were in hysterics. Didi climbed onto a branch above me and delicately caressed my head, gently running her fingers through my hair.

"No insects," she said. "No good!"

I carefully tapped her far shoulder and she fell for it, urgently looking over to see what had touched her.

I was having so much fun, but there were hundreds of questions whizzing around in my head, and I didn't have much time.

"Shalan, can you tell me more about monkey magic? Why does it not work on other humans, so you can get more help? Why just me?"

Shalan raised his arm, and the adults stopped playing. Nina and Didi gripped each other and rolled around like a furry ginger ball.

"Nobody really knows," Shalan said. "Forest decides when magic comes and who gets moonlight power. Forest knows when magic needed. I only seeing monkey magic once before."

"When was that?"

"After big fire."

"What happened after the fire?"

Shalan did not answer and pointed to the sky. "Moon gets lower," he said. "Time to go."

He was right. The magic would wear off without moonlight. "Remember: follow the Cyclops," said Shalan, as Larnie beckoned me to follow her back.

I had completely forgotten about that. I would ask Dad in the morning. All I knew about a Cyclops was that it was a one-eyed monster. I didn't fancy meeting one, let alone following it.

Back at the lodge, Larnie waved goodbye and sprang from the window as I climbed into bed.

\* \* \*

I woke up startled and wondered again whether I had been dreaming. The missing bottles and fruit reassured me that the experience was real. I lay thinking about the boat and the men in the forest, trying to work out what was happening. Why was Dr Nazir watching the sea at night?

Still unable to sleep, I crept out the door to go to the toilet. Daylight was breaking, and I glanced down the main track to the start of the sacred path. Where did it lead?

No harm in having a look, I thought, and I tiptoed over.

The path was almost dead straight and headed steeply down, shrouded in dense greenery. I took a few paces along and looked around to make sure I hadn't fallen into the pits of hell. Phew, not yet at least. I decided to go on.

Then something transfixed me: it was moving way ahead of me. I walked quickly to catch up and could make out a person. For an instant I was petrified, thinking it might be the boy's ghost. But this was no boy; it was clearly an adult.

He or she was dragging a huge sack.

Was it the person who had dived from the top of the forest canopy?

I shouted, "Hello. Are you okay?"

The person kept walking, but so slowly that I was catching up easily. I suddenly felt afraid. What was I doing, chasing a stranger down a sacred path that might lead to hell? But my legs wouldn't stop, and soon I was no more than ten paces away.

It was then that the stranger heard me. Tall and muscular for someone so old, he was clearly a man. He stopped and lowered his heavy bag, his wild grey hair blowing in the breeze.

He took what seemed like minutes to turn.

I gasped as I saw his face.

He had just one eye. Like a Cyclops.

## Chapter 6

# SKULL PATH

"Don't be scared," the one-eyed man said.

"Who are you?" I asked, frightened but curious. Follow the Cyclops, the orangutan had commanded. Here he was.

"I am Mohamed. I am a man of peace."

"But I saw you jumping from the treetops today. Are you all right?"

"I have many talents, but not walking on treetops, young lady."

"I don't understand."

"You will, you will. Are you coming to save the orangutans?" His voice was gentle and caring, not what you'd imagine from someone who looked as if he had stepped straight out of a horror movie. He wore ragged trousers and a faded khaki shirt.

"Where are you going?" I asked.

"Not far now. Near where you saw me skydiving this

morning. I know this forest like the back of my hand. Follow me."

"Do you live here?" I asked, walking a pace or two behind him.

"I used to be the warden."

So this was the madman Anton had warned us about. He didn't seem so crazy – maybe just a little crazy.

"What's in that sack?" I asked.

"Bananas, orange, papaya, mango: orangutan dinner!"

"So you feed them?"

"Someone has to. Look at their forest. It's disappearing."

Almost at that exact moment, the path opened onto a vast clearing, and the line of thick rainforest came to an abrupt end. Branches with yellow leaves were scattered as far as I could see. In between, small palm trees were growing in piles of fresh soil, as if they had only just been planted.

"This is where I do my skydiving," the old warden laughed. He turned his sack upside down and emptied a giant pile of fruit onto the ground. I walked over to one of the saplings and noticed a tag on it: a small piece of green paper with a palm tree and the letter M. It was the same logo that I had seen on the barge two nights ago.

"Did the apes send you?" the warden asked.

I jumped. I hadn't heard him creep up behind me. His eye stared spookily at me, next to a chunk of scarred skin where his other eye should be and probably once was.

"The apes told me to follow you. How do you know?"

"You know the answer now. You must help them."

"What answer? I'm confused."

"Confusion leads to clarity," he said. "Just stay off Skull Path. You hear?"

Great, I thought. Nothing was clear. And what or where was Skull Path?

But then he was gone. I looked around and couldn't see where he had disappeared to. Just like Danny, Mohamed was there one second and nowhere the next.

I thought I recognized the path we had arrived on and began following it back to the jungle. About ten minutes later I knew that this wasn't the way I had come.

I looked up as the sun rose above the treetops. My vision went blurry from the light but I trudged on. Then I tripped on a root, falling to my knees. There were some huge rocks next to the path; I got up and walked towards them. There was something creepy about the rocks, and then it dawned on me. One boulder had two great holes in it, like eye sockets. Another rock immediately below had a long, mouth-shaped gap. Together, they looked like a skull.

This was Skull Path.

I walked on nervously, staring at the rocks, then felt the crunch of dried palm leaves below my feet. I took another step but this time there was no crunch as my foot passed straight through the leaves and I tumbled. Dropping for what felt like seconds, I knew I had fallen into a trap. I plunged three metres, perhaps four, crashing to the ground so hard that I was winded and bruised. Catching my breath, I stretched my limbs; luckily no bones were broken. I was in a pit, a dark pit covered at the top by the palm leaves.

A moment later I was startled by some movement. There was something else in the pit with me. Not a wild cat, please! Or a snake!

Then my companions in the pit emerged from a dark corner, and I couldn't believe my luck: it was Larnie, holding Nina and Didi. I gave them a hug and did a mini-hula dance. Unlike the past two nights, I couldn't understand their grunts – and Larnie was certainly grunting, making lots of noise. No moonlight, no monkey magic, I understood. It would have to wait until the moon rose.

It took me just a few more seconds to realize that something terrible had happened. That was why Larnie was so upset. Didi was shoving Nina, urging her to play, but there was no reaction. Nina's eyes stared blankly, and her arms flopped limply over her mother's shoulder. Was she sick again?

Then I noticed the blood running from her head. She must have hurt herself falling into the pit. Larnie's eyes were full of tears, and she stared at me, pleading for help.

I pulled water out of my knapsack and poured some over Nina's lips.

Voices from above stopped me. Palm leaves covered all but the edge of the opening I had fallen through, so it was hard to make out the conversation until they were just above us. What I heard was chilling.

"Boss man gives me fifty dollar for live monkey and twenty dollar for dead one. Easier to kill and take twenty bucks than fight the stupid furry things."

Another man laughed.

"Doctor man from England here so boss say don't use gun. Poison gas slower and more pain but less noisy."

"Or fire," said the other. "There's no mistaking monkey skull, even burnt one." Their stomach-turning laughter got quieter as they walked away.

Nina was now laid out on the floor, Larnie stroking her head and Didi still urging her sister to play. I began sobbing. There was no doubt that it was too late: poor, fun Nina.

A blue piece of paper on the ground caught my eye; it looked like one of Dad's business cards. I picked it up and froze. There was a picture of a palm tree and a letter M – just like on the sapling and on the barge.

Next to the logo were the words: Mukada Palm Oil.

"Operations chief" and a phone number were written below, though unlike most business cards there was no name.

I slipped the card in my back pocket and sat with my arm around Larnie, both of us in tears. Didi refused to believe anything was wrong with her sister and kept doing hulas and prodding Nina for a reaction. There was none.

## Chapter 7

# SLEEP

Almost in an instant, everything became clear. In a way, it was obvious. Everyone knew what humans had being doing for years to harm orangutans, to cause their numbers to dwindle.

Orangutans spend almost their entire lives in trees. With no forest, they have no place to live. For decades, humans had been chopping down the rainforests to sell the timber and plant money-making trees or crops. Dad said that for every five acres of orangutan habitat, four had already been destroyed. Mukada Nature Reserve was becoming the latest graveyard for orangutans.

The barge I had seen was transporting trees that had been chopped down and would be sold. The men were planting palm trees to produce expensive palm oil. The orangutans were being forced to the coast because their environment was being devastated; they had nowhere else to go.

The men dragging branches were part of the scheme. From very high in the sky, the branches looked like treetops – an attempt to fool Dad in the helicopter. Except some were old and had already turned yellow. I hoped Dad had figured it out. And Mohamed hadn't jumped from the treetops. He had been walking among the branches and simply dived to the ground when he heard the helicopter.

Dr Nazir must be involved, too. He hadn't wanted us in the helicopter. And also I'd seen him at the river mouth; surely he knew what was going on.

Perhaps I was chosen for monkey magic because of my knowledge of orangutans. Perhaps there was no reason, and I had just been in Mukada at the right time – or wrong time, depending on how you looked at it. I doubted I would ever fully understand monkey magic – where it came from, why it only worked in moonlight, how it allowed me to understand the apes. But if Shalan was right, I was here for a purpose.

My moonlit escapades had helped achieve the first goal: discovering why the orangutans were suffering and losing their habitat. The next part – doing something about it – seemed an impossible task as I sat in the pit staring at Didi desperately poking Nina for signs of life.

How was I going to let Dad know? And what were those men at the top of the pit planning? Poison or fire to kill Larnie and Didi? I dreaded to think what might happen if they attempted that.

Soon their voices came closer again. "Boss says Englishman knowing too much. We may need to deal with – "

A shout interrupted them. "Romy! Romy!"

It was Dad! I was about to shout back but stopped myself; I couldn't say anything as the men would hear me. They probably had guns and could harm us. I desperately wanted to reply but could not put us – or Dad – at risk.

"Romy, where are you?" he shouted.

What could I do? A single tear dribbled down my right cheek. "Romy! Are you there?" His voice faded into the distance. "Romy!"

The men were whispering now. I prayed they weren't going to follow Dad. Please go away, Dad, fast!

His voice faded, and soon theirs, too, disappeared.

Didi had by now stopped prodding Nina. A ray of sunlight pierced a gap in the branches covering the pit, illuminating Nina's face. A fly landed on one of her closed eyes, and I soon realized there were swarms buzzing around her body. I swatted the air, but it made little difference as the flies sensed an easy meal. Didi snuggled into Larnie's arms in a dark corner of the damp pit, both a picture of sadness.

I had never felt so low. The air in the pit was hot, stale and damp, Dad was in danger, I was trapped, and Nina was gone. Maybe the locals were right, and this was hell.

There was a rustle from above and I gasped, expecting to see something terrible. Instead, a familiar, toothy grin poked over the edge.

It was Danny, dangling a rope. My hero, Danny!

"Shhh!" he implored. "Idiot men close."

Larnie climbed the rope in an instant, gripping her two children under one arm and making it look easy. I began pulling myself up while trying to find footholds in the mud. I lost my grip and felt a sharp burning pain as my hands tightened on the rope. The moist air made it harder to breathe, and I was gasping and had sweat running down my face by the time I had struggled to the top.

"Quick, follow!" Danny commanded.

Larnie disappeared into the trees with her infants, and I crawled behind Danny through thick vegetation. After five minutes he was satisfied that we were clear of danger, and got up and began walking. I did the same. Within twenty minutes we were at the lodge. It was deserted. Where was Dad?

"Father in danger," Danny said, holding my hand and staring into my eyes with his kind, intense eyes. He wiped a tear from my cheek. "I go help. Wait for now. Best hide."

"I will come," I said.

"Wait, Romy!"

"I must come."

"You must stay. I will come back."

"Well, you must take this." I unclipped the blue lapis lazuli necklace and handed it to him. He nodded his thanks, slipped it into his pocket and ran off into the forest. I quickly lost sight of him, but noticed a piece of paper under a rock on the table.

DEAR ROMY
CALL ANTON WITH
SATELLITE PHONE UNDER
PILLOW: NUMBER IS
6345679. PROMISE
WE'LL BE OK HULA GIRL!
LOVE DAD

I dashed into our room, which was empty except for a few of my things. I lifted Dad's pillow: nothing. I looked under my pillow, Anton's pillow, but no phone. Someone had taken it.

I was alone.

Frightened, I shouted for Dad outside until my throat hurt, but there was no answer. I walked down the sacred path, wiping sweat from my brow, but saw nobody. Returning to the lodge at dusk, I sat on my bed wondering what to do. Where was Danny? He had warned me Dad was in trouble; then he just vanished. And what about Anton? Was he also in danger?

It was too late to walk back to the main lodge at the beach. There was only one option: I had to fall asleep and hope for monkey magic. I lay on the bed in the darkness, my body exhausted but my mind full of energy. It was like the night of Christmas Eve; I desperately wanted to sleep, but the more I tried, the harder it became. Sleep is something you drift into, not charge at. I strained to think of blackness, but instead of soothing, sparkling shapes, this time I saw the Mukada Palm Oil logo and poor Nina lying still, the life squeezed from her small body.

After trying to sleep for an hour, I felt more restless than ever. Then the idea came to me: when I was younger I used to cuddle Robbie, my toy orangutan, to comfort me, to make me sleep. I grabbed Dad's pillow and imagined that it was Robbie. It seemed to work; I immediately relaxed as I hugged the soft monkey-pillow. My body felt lighter, my mind less busy, my thoughts slowed, and blackness overcame me.

Tap-tap on my shoulder!

I opened my eyes.

"You late," said Dunga. "Great danger at Mukada."

# Chapter 8

# MUKADA

Dunga leapt through the window and into the trees. He swung twice as fast as Larnie, and I lost my grip straining to keep up, only breaking my fall by grabbing another branch at the last moment. The thought of Dad in danger filled me with energy – fierce and determined energy. The top of the canopy looked like a strange landscape in the moonlight and then I noticed how low the moon was. There wasn't much time before the magic would disappear.

"Hurry," Dunga shouted. "Mukada not far."

My arms were beginning to ache, and the toe I had stubbed two nights ago was throbbing. But I kept going until Dunga stopped on an orangutan nest halfway up the canopy. He held his right hand in the air and stared at me with his friendly eyes.

"Father no hear you because monkey magic," Dunga said. "He see and hear orangutan instead."

That didn't stop me screaming his name as I looked down onto a wooden shack. He was sat on a rocking chair on the veranda at the front, his hands tied behind the chair. I screamed again. Dad looked up, his knapsack by his feet, and I waved.

"No see you," Dunga repeated. "Just see orangutan."

"We must help him."

"We help."

The old shack was submerged in jungle, with branches growing along the sides as if trying to swallow it. We were almost directly above Dad. As we watched, the door swung open and out walked a man, dressed in a red cape, with a hideous face. He had great white fangs and bulging eyes. One of the teeth glistened gold. It was a terrifying mask.

"So will you accept my offer?" the masked man screamed. "We save the Os and ship them to zoos, reserves – whatever – if you keep quiet about our business."

"Your business here is killing them," Dad shouted. "And why should I believe you? Why should I do what you ask?"

"There will be a large cash deposit in your bank account to remind you how you made the right decision," the masked man bellowed in an absurd, monstrous voice.

He sounded like he was putting on the accent, like a bad actor in a play. Perhaps he did not want to be recognized, or perhaps he really was some sort of monster.

"I'll never accept your dirty money," Dad replied. "And you should know that I compiled a report about the logging operation. It will be sent to everyone I know in one week's time via email. I did it in case something happened. Now, for the last time, where is Romy? If you bring her, I will stop the email."

"So who's in charge here?" the masked man shouted. He picked up Dad's knapsack and ripped out a computer. He held it in the air and threw it off the veranda.

"That won't stop the e – " Dad stopped.

The man hurled the bag in anger and stormed into the shack. He came out with a fuel can and poured liquid over the computer. Striking a match, he shouted: "Your report is history."

He struck a match and dropped it onto the laptop. The flames jumped as though awoken angrily. Dad turned his head over his shoulder to shield himself. The flames grew and caressed the overhanging roof.

"We must do something," I pleaded.

Dunga held up his hand to stop me.

The roof was now alight. The flames crept around the top of the shack and then seemed to speed up, hungry to devour everything. The wooden steps leading up to the veranda were smouldering.

"This could have been easier, you fool," the masked man said. "Your daughter will suffer now." He jumped over the wooden railing of the veranda onto the path, the demonic eyes of the mask staring madly, and ran off. He had left Dad to burn.

Dad was coughing now, his beard hopefully filtering some of the billowing, suffocating smoke. The flames surrounded him. I could not just sit by and watch.

"Wait," Dunga told me. "This is Mukada."

He was suddenly gone.

There was so much smoke that I could barely see what happened next. A giant branch fell towards my father under the weight of something large. The branch bent until it hovered just above him; out came an outstretched orange arm. Another branch tipped over above Dad's head and an orangutan leapt into the inferno. It was Dunga! He grappled with the rope tying Dad's hands. Seconds later, Dad was holding his hands to his mouth, coughing. From the other overhanging branch, the arm grabbed Dad's hand and lifted him into the air. Dad was huge in comparison, but the

orangutan's strength was enough to drag him to safety.

It was just as Danny had described in his story about the Curse of Mukada, except for one difference.

To my horror, Dunga jumped onto the very top of the roof, the only part yet to be engulfed in flames. He held something in the air with his arms extended, as if making an offering. I couldn't make it out at first. Then the smoke gusted in a different direction, and I caught a glimpse.

It was an infant orangutan.

It was Nina!

He cried something that I couldn't hear because of the noisy flames and placed the body on the roof. Danny's face flashed through my mind, and I recalled him on the first night at the base, explaining that death had to be repaid for the curse to be broken. Was this what was happening? Would Nina's body make amends for the death of the boy?

The fire surrounded Dunga now, and he thrust his long orange arm upwards, where another orangutan grasped him and tried to lift him into the trees. The two apes lost their grip on each other, and Dunga tumbled onto the flaming roof.

I couldn't let this happen. I couldn't let him perish. He'd saved my father. I grabbed a bendy branch in front of me and jumped with my right arm, straining to reach Dunga. It felt like I was falling off a roof, until the branch reached its limit and slowed me to a stop just above the fire.

The scalding heat pierced me like an arrow. I bounced back before coming down again and somehow clutched his hand. Dunga was coughing, and the fur on his back smoked, but I summoned all my strength and yanked him hard. I don't know where I got the power, but Dunga held onto my arm and another orangutan pulled us both up and away from the flames.

We scrambled to the nest, where Dad lay coughing. I hugged him and put an arm around him. He looked at me strangely, like he had never met me. Then I remembered: monkey magic. He saw an orangutan, not his daughter. I didn't care. I kept hugging him with all the love in my soul. Larnie was watching us sadly. I knew she was grieving over Nina. She grabbed Didi and embraced her remaining daughter. Dunga coughed and put an arm around his family, while Shalan sat nearby, shaking his head. The other orangutan, the one that had pulled me and Dunga to safety, looked at me, and I noticed a cut or mark on his left foot. I didn't have time to thank him as he turned and jumped into the trees. Then a loud fizzing burst into the sky and startled everyone. Suddenly the whole forest turned bright red. The orangutans were scared, but Dad chuckled. This strange scene – orangutans, my father perched on a nest high in the rainforest, the fire raging below – was now painted bright red.

"My flare," Dad said to himself. "I always carry a flare in my knapsack."

"Sky turn red," Shalan cried. "Sky turn blood red!"

"Sky turn blood red!" Larnie repeated excitedly.

So that was why they had left Nina's body on the roof:

they were attempting to break the curse of Mukada.

"Death is repaid, and sky turn blood red at Mukada," Dunga said solemnly.

To Dad, their voices were just grunts, I knew. He rested his head and closed his eyes, exhausted. We watched the shack burning, and I noticed the chair Dad had been strapped to glowing bright orange. How close he had been to losing his life. The orangutans had saved him.

"What is strange noise?" Dunga asked me.

"It's called snoring."

Didi made a snoring noise and everyone laughed, even Larnie. Didi leant over and pretended to pull something from Dad's beard, shoving it in her mouth.

"He grow banana in there," Didi squeaked, again prompting laughter.

"We must take him back," Larnie interrupted. "Before monkey magic stop."

"What about the masked man?" I asked.

"We take care him," Dunga replied. "We get him at Skull Path."

## Chapter 9

# TRAPPED

I woke up on the forest floor with Dad next to me. The daylight confirmed to me that the monkey magic had passed. We were on the sacred path, no more than 200 metres from the main track and the forest lodge. Dad was still snoring and smelled of smoke. I held him tightly. Then I remembered we were still in grave danger.

I gave a nudge, and Dad opened his eyes slowly. He smothered me in a huge bear hug. "Thank goodness you are safe," he whispered. "That was the strangest night." He started to tell me, but I stopped him.

"I know what happened. The fire, the masked man, the orangutans saving you. I know everything."

He looked startled. "But how? Were you there?"

"It's hard to explain, but yes. What happened to Anton?"

"I've no idea. We went searching for you yesterday and some men jumped us. They took Anton off kicking and screaming and dragged me to this shack in the forest – well it sounds like you know the rest."

"Who was the man in the mask?"

"I don't know, but he tried to kill me."

It wasn't over yet, I thought. Our plane wasn't due to arrive for another four days. We had to find Anton in case he was hurt or in trouble. I was itching to see Danny, too.

Dad told me he had suspected what was going on – the logging, the destruction of the rainforest – but he had no proof. I told him then about the barge, the men dragging branches, the sapling palms being planted; he had the proof now.

We just needed to get away before we were caught. With nowhere to go, that was easier said than done.

\* \* \*

The cigarette smell reached us at about the same time as the voices: they were looking for us and were close.

We kept as near to the track as possible, to make sure we didn't get lost, but far enough away so as not to be spotted. We had passed the forest lodge and, as expected, people were waiting there in case we returned. They had guns.

The voices were directly in front of us now, not from the track. Then there were voices behind us, too. They were all around us; we had to hide.

Then we heard another noise.

"Psst! Psst!"

From behind a tree emerged a man with wild grey hair – a man with just one eye. "Follow me," he said.

"It's the old warden," I whispered to Dad. "He's all right. I think."

The voices were getting closer, the cigarette smell stronger.

"Ok, let's go," Dad said.

We had been following the old warden for no more than five minutes when he leaned over and pulled palm leaves off the ground. He climbed into a hole. We jumped in behind him, and he put the leaves back to cover the opening.

"Welcome to my home," he whispered. The pit was no

bigger than a prison cell.

There was a mattress made of dry leaves in the corner and a huge pile of books, but little else. We sat on the floor, and he offered us some water and fruit. We were starving and devoured the succulent mango and soft banana.

The voices had gone by the time we finished eating.

"Why are you living like this in the forest?" Dad asked.

"The forest was always my home," Mohamed said. "I guess you could say I am married to the Mukada Nature Reserve. She is the love of my life, my family, and I am just another one of the endangered species here."

He laughed.

"And it's not just me and the orangutans," he continued. "The sun bear, proboscis monkey, clouded leopard, the Borneo elephant and rhinoceros, countless species of plants – they all face extinction because of these greedy people."

"But, Mohamed, why did you lose your job?" Dad asked. "You are exactly the kind of person they need here."

"I asked too many questions about the trees disappearing. It has always gone on but it started getting worse after they ran out of forest elsewhere and turned to the national parks. I wrote to the newspapers when nobody would listen, but they took my passport and money, threatened to kill me if I spoke out. It was easy for them to brush me off as a madman. All they had to do was show everyone a picture and people believed it."

He lowered his head, closed his eye for a couple of

seconds and suddenly opened it wide, staring at me, then began laughing.

"You see?" he smiled.

I did my best not to flinch.

"That's terrible," I said, feeling ashamed that I too had judged this wonderful man by his appearance at first. "But you could at least comb your hair! It does make you look a little crazy."

Mohamed laughed again.

"I've given up caring what people think," he said. "I am getting old and I just want to devote my life to feeding the monkeys and apes."

Mohamed explained that he had lost his job months before Dr Nazir took over and had never known the new warden.

"But I ask this," Mohamed continued. "Who would work all their life for nature only to end up destroying it? It doesn't make sense that he is behind this."

"It seems odd," said Dad. "But money talks."

"He has other things on his mind, not money," Mohamed said. "He goes to the river every night."

"He is checking the barges, the ones taking the forest away," I said. "I watched him."

"So from confusion comes clarity!" Mohamed said. "Well done, young girl, but not total clarity. He is not there to watch those boats come and go."

"What is he doing then?" I asked.

"The ferry arrives from the mainland once a day, in the

middle of the night. He waits for his loved ones. His wife suddenly left last year without saying where she was going, and he awaits her and the child's return every night. His heart is broken."

"At least Danny is here," I said.

"I thought she took the boy with her," Mohamed said. "But I know Danny. I've talked to him."

"Romy, are you sure?" asked Dad. "Nobody else has seen Danny."

"Of course I'm sure."

More than ever, I wanted Danny to make one of his mysterious appearances, to show them I was right, but also because I wanted to see him, to talk with him. He was my friend.

Mohamed held up his hand. There were more cigarette fumes from above us.

We sat in silence and I thought about what Mohamed had said about Dr Nazir's broken heart. But surely if he went to the river, Dr Nazir would know about the barges – the boats shipping the timber with their Mukada Palm Oil logo. And why did the masked man have a golden tooth, like Dr Nazir? Was that a coincidence?

The voices began shouting, but something drowned them out. The whir of helicopter blades grew louder, and soon it was directly above our heads. It sounded like they had found us. What were they going to do? Dad put his arm around me. I gripped his hand tight.

The chopper circled above us, and then another joined in. There was a third helicopter. I looked up, and through the palm leaves saw them hovering like eagles searching for prey.

"Excellent!" said Dad, also staring at the sky.

What could be excellent about this?

He stood up and climbed out of the pit. "Don't worry," he turned to me. "We're going to be okay, like I promised."

Then he started waving his arms furiously.

"Do you need this?" the old warden asked, passing him a tube with a string hanging from it. "Brilliant," Dad said. He yanked the string and a red flare shot into the sky. Was he going mad?

"There is a clearing over there," Mohamed added, pointing. Dad grabbed my hand and pulled me out of the pit. We ran to the clearing and I looked up: there were now ten helicopters at least.

"It's hula time," Dad shouted. "I emailed a report yesterday to the authorities. They're not trying to capture us; they're trying to save us."

"So that email, the one you were going to send next week?"

"That was a bluff. I already sent it. Thank goodness."

My blond hair, a little smellier than usual, went berserk from the rotor wash as one of the helicopters landed and the door swung open. We clambered in. A man in army uniform shook Dad's hand and patted me on the shoulder. There was no sign of the people who had followed us. Mohamed had also disappeared, probably back to his humble pit to prepare the next batch of fruit for his beloved orangutans.

"Do you have a satellite phone?" Dad asked the uniformed man. "I think I can remember Anton's number."

The army man pulled a telephone from the front of the helicopter and handed it to Dad.

"Here," I said, pushing my fingers into my pocket to clutch the note Dad had written to me, the one with Anton's number on it. The blue business card fell out of my pocket at the same time as I handed the scrunched-up paper over and Dad keyed in Anton's number.

I looked down at the card.

Then it suddenly struck me.

I checked the paper in Dad's hand again to make sure: the number on the business card and the number on the note from Dad were exactly the same: Anton's phone number was on the business card for Mukada Palm Oil.

Then I remembered the masked man screaming at Dad the previous night. He had called orangutans "Os." That was also how Anton spoke about them. It all started to make sense. Anton had lied about the winds on our helicopter ride. He had taken us over the part of the forest where the branches were laid, then suddenly abandoned the trip before we got a chance to see the rest of the Mukada Nature Reserve. Dad had sensed something was wrong.

It wasn't Dr Nazir behind this; it was his assistant.

Anton was the Operations Chief of the company destroying the rainforest.

Dad dialled the number, and it rang fifteen times before somebody answered frantically. He screamed in a European accent: "Help! Help! The apes, the apes, get me out of here! They are throwing – ouch!"

Then the phone cut out.

We took off, and I stared into the forest at the treetops that were yellow yesterday and had since turned brown. We flew over the golden beach where we had first arrived. The pig was still munching on grass. Someone was waving: it was Danny! I waved back, but he was gone before I had time to show Dad.

# Chapter 10

# HULA TIME

Just like Dunga had said, the police found Anton that night on Skull Path, cowering in the corner of the same pit I had fallen into. His bag contained a red cape and a mask with a golden tooth. Strangely, he was smothered in mashed-up fruit and covered in bruises. They said he was in shock and wouldn't speak about what had happened between leaving the fire and being discovered in the pit.

At his trial, Anton shook his head nervously when asked about it and muttered something about a boy turning into an orangutan and bombarding him with a sackful of fruit. Everyone thought he was mad. Anton was sentenced to jail, but was out within six months and back working for Mukada Palm Oil. The company was fined – not much, according to Dad – and forced to make a donation towards orangutan conservation. That was part of the problem, Dad said: people continued to get away with destroying the rainforest.

Dr Nazir was fired as chief warden but wasn't charged by police. He had been guilty of not doing his job properly, nothing more. Devastated by his wife's departure, he had let Anton run the reserve with such dire results. He soon left Borneo to find his family.

Back in London, I often thought about Danny: the way he appeared from nowhere, his smooth skin and rugged feet with the S-shaped scar, the way he saved us on Skull Path. I also thought about the orangutans and how their habitat had been shattered. I went back to hugging Robbie every night and – you know what? – I found it easier to get to sleep.

When I was younger, I had spent a whole year asking for a snowman in London; now my only wish was to see orangutans back in the rainforest Anton had destroyed. Dad promised me that the orangutans would return to Mukada one day. But that was one promise I couldn't see him keeping.

* * *

I had known about the destruction of rainforests before the trip, but the experience of seeing it firsthand, especially watching Nina perish, had brought home the seriousness of the situation.

I spent most of my spare time at school researching orangutans, proboscis monkeys and other endangered animals, and got an ovation from my class when I presented a project on the rainforests of Borneo. I gave talks to other classes and sent letters to powerful people pleading for them to do something about the disappearing forests. Some of them replied and said they would help.

I even got my picture in the newspaper for arranging a fund-raising fair in the local park. Dad dressed up as an orangutan, and we had entertainers, including jugglers and conjurers.

The newspaper headline was: Monkey Magic!

It was frustrating not being able to tell everyone why that was such a coincidence. Keeping monkey magic secret had been incredibly hard. I was dying to tell my friends and parents, but what could I say? They'd think I was mad, too. I thought about explaining it to Dad when he asked how I had watched the orangutans save his life. My explanation – that Danny had taken me to Mukada – seemed to satisfy him, at least for now.

Dad was away a lot in the months after we returned, though he never really talked about his projects, changing the subject whenever Mum or I asked. Then one day, about a week before the spring holidays, he told me we were going on another trip. I was excited, but nothing like the last time – until he revealed we were returning to Borneo then heading to China for another assignment.

\* \* \*

We landed on the same grey, pot-holed airstrip as before, in the same rickety plane. There, waiting for us, was Mohamed, now back in his old job running the reserve and wearing a rather fetching black leather eyepatch and – guess what – khakis. We drove straight to the beach lodge along a new widened track and headed into what was left of the forest, pulling up outside a brand-new building with a freshly painted sign: the Mukada Sanctuary.

"This is what's been keeping me busy," Dad said, proudly stroking his beard. "I wanted it to be a surprise."

We walked past the building, and all around us were trees teeming with life, teeming with orangutans! It was only a small part of what used to be the rainforest, but it was a home for my favourite animals. At least it was somewhere for them to live until the rainforest recovered.

"There you go, Romy," Dad said. "So what if there's no rainforest left in Mukada? I promised you we'd see orangutans here again."

\* \* \*

We sat around a table at lunch, eating succulent mango and melon and talking about Mohamed's plans for the nature reserve and the sanctuary. I was dying to ask about Danny, and finally plucked up the courage.

"Did you ever see Dr Nazir's son?"

"Oh, yes, I remember you saying you saw him," Mohamed

replied. "But Romy, I never did. Just out of interest, was he carrying his white stick?"

"White stick? He isn't blind."

"But Danny Nazir is blind. That is one reason they say the wife left – it was too hard on the boy being here without his sight. I've only got one eye, and it's tricky enough, believe me."

My friend Danny most certainly was not blind. I felt a chill run through my body. Then I remembered meeting Danny on my first day at the forest base, when we introduced each other. I asked him if he was called Danny. He said I could call him Danny if I liked.

He had never said he was Danny!

I thought about the rest of our conversation that night, when he had described the curse. I wanted to learn more about it from Mohamed.

"Have you heard of the curse of Mukada?" I asked.

"Of course," he replied. "Maybe the boy finally has peace."

Again, I felt a shiver. Hadn't the boy died in the flames?

"What do you mean?" I asked.

He then told the story just as Danny had, with the orangutans saving the village, only the ending was different.

The child left by the orangutans didn't burn to death, Mohamed said, but was found in the trees six months later. He had been cared for by orangutans all that time. He returned to his parents, but they would not accept him because he couldn't speak like the other children and he looked so wild. To the parents, the son they brought up had died, Mohamed explained, his voice now full of sorrow and his eye tearful.

"Their other son was badly hurt in the fire, so they took out their anger with the curse," he sighed. "The brother tried to persuade the boy to come home, but the boy was taunted by the other kids and so he refused to return. Having received love and compassion from the orangutans, he desperately wanted to become one. But he was trapped inside the body of a boy.

"The moonlight has special powers though," Mohamed continued. "And he could take the form of a monkey or an ape at night, according to the legend. Monkey magic, they called it. He never aged either, because the power from the moonlight preserves youth and he would transform every night. Or so the story goes."

Oh my goodness! Had I been stuck at eleven years and seven months for the past few months? I reassured myself with the thought that I had only spent three nights swinging through the trees. Also, I had grown into bigger-sized shoes since then.

"According to the story," Mohamed went on, "he would only find peace when the curse was broken: when death was repaid and the orangutans began flourishing again in Mukada."

"How much of this do you believe?" Dad asked.

"Some of it is true," he answered. "The orangutans have certainly suffered under the curse. And the curse definitely exists."

"How can you be so sure?" I inquired. Nothing had prepared me for his reply. I almost fell off my seat.

"Because I was there when my parents invoked the curse."

"Your parents!" I cried, my eyes and mouth wide open. "So the boy was your brother?"

"Yes, Khalid was my brother," Mohamed replied. "I, too, was a young boy when the fire destroyed Mukada. The apes saved my life, but a burning branch gouged my face. That night, I lost my eye – and I lost my brother."

\* \* \*

Dad showed me around the sanctuary that afternoon: the incubators for the newborn apes, the hospice for sick orangutans and fruit-laden nests for the rest. Most of the orangutans would be taken to rainforests in other parts of Borneo as soon as they were over their illnesses and ready for the wild.

I borrowed Dad's binoculars and scanned the trees for Dunga, Didi, Larnie or Shalan. After so many months, I wasn't sure I'd recognize them; Didi would have grown so much. I kept thinking about Khalid and the curse of Mukada. It all seemed so farfetched. But after what had happened to me in

Mukada, I believed almost anything was possible.

A lorry started its engine at the front of the sanctuary and I noticed a huge cage full of orangutans on the back. I walked over and peeked in at seven beautiful apes, all heading for new lives. I prayed they would adapt to wherever they were going.

Something caught my eye. It was bright blue and glistening. I looked closely, and saw that one of the orangutans was holding the sparkling object: a blue lapis lazuli necklace, the one Mum had given me. The orangutan must have found it in the forest.

The creature stared down at me from the truck. I walked closer and looked into his human-like eyes. The orangutan stretched out an arm, and I turned my head away, scared at first. But the ape tickled my chin, and I looked down to see a pink flower in his hand.

In shock, I noticed a scar on his foot. It was in the same place as the marking on the orangutan that had dragged me and Dunga out of the flames at Mukada.

My eyes were suddenly full of tears.

The scar was shaped like a snake. The orangutan stretched both arms to one side and started wobbling its hips.

"It's hula time, Khalid," I whispered, tears running down my cheeks, tears of sorrow and of joy.

# Interesting facts About Orangutans

• Our close relationship with orangutans is reflected in the name: orangutan means "man of the forest".

• Orangutans live in Malaysia and Indonesia, on the islands of Borneo and Sumatra, in Southeast Asia. In 1900, more than 300,000 of these apes roamed the forests. Now there are only 50,000 to 60,000. The main reason for their demise is the loss of their habitat, caused by humans.

• Fewer than 8,000 orangutans now live in Sumatra. These apes are smaller and have lighter and longer hair than Borneo's orangutans.

• Orangutans can live as long as 60 years. Males weigh up to 100 kg (220 pounds) and stand 1.2 to 1.4 metres tall (4 to 4.7 feet); females weigh as much as 50 kg (110 pounds) and grow to 1 to 1.2 metres (3.3 to 4 feet) in height.

• Orangutans stay with their mothers until they are about seven years old. Unlike the ape families depicted in *Monkey Magic*, real orangutan fathers have little to do with their families.

• Orangutans' arms are twice as long as their legs. They use both arms and legs while foraging for food. Orangutans with the big pads on their faces are male and are called "flanged".

• Orangutans build a new nest to sleep in virtually every night.

• Fruit makes up more than half of the orangutan diet. They love figs and durian – a spiky, green fruit whose smell is so pungent it is banned from many buildings in Singapore. They also eat young leaves, shoots, seeds, bark, insects and bird eggs. In desperation, they may even munch on soil or feed on small animals such as birds.

• Orangutans, some researchers say, are the most intelligent animal other than humans. Studies have shown they are capable of using leaves to make rain hats and leakproof roofs over their nests. Adults have been observed teaching youngsters how to make tools and find food.

• Orangutans from Borneo are listed as "endangered" by the World Conservation Union. Sumatran orangutans are listed as "critically endangered".

• Very few wild orangutans will be left in two decades unless the destruction of the rainforests, mostly through illegal logging, is halted. The situation may be worse than that, even: many of the last refuges for orangutans, including national parks, might be decimated by 2012, leaving the apes nowhere to go, according to a United Nations report.

• The UN report found that the rainforests containing orangutans were being cleared so rapidly that almost all will be destroyed by 2022 unless "urgent action" is taken. Satellite photography reveals that loggers are now ripping down rainforests in most of Indonesia's national parks.

• The UN report also said orangutans are often killed for meat or to protect newly planted crops.

• About 1,000 orangutans are poached from the wild every year, often for sale as pets.

• Ah Meng, one of the world's most famous orangutans, was originally a pet. She spent most of her life in Singapore Zoo and was the only non-human to be awarded Singapore's "Special Tourism Ambassador" award. She appeared in films promoting Singapore and, like many movie stars, could be temperamental. Once, while filming, she climbed a tree and refused to come down for three days. Following her death at age 48 in 2008, 4000 people showed up to pay their respects. Newspapers around the world carried her obituary.

• The Bornean orangutan Ken Allen was a well-known escape artist at the San Diego Zoo. He unscrewed bolts and climbed steep walls to get out of his cage, only to be found among zoo visitors and led by the hand to a keeper. His admirers started a Ken Allen fan club and wrote songs about him. He died in 2000.

• For teacher worksheet downloads about conservation, orangutans, *Monkey Magic* and writing, visit the "School Stuff" section at www.monkeymagicbook.com.

 If you have a smartphone, the QR code here will take you to exclusive online content about Monkey Magic direct from the printed page. Here's how to do it. **1.** Go online using your phone, enter 'QR code reader' into a search engine or app store. **2.** Find a compatible application for your phone. **3.** Download and install the free app. **4.** Launch the app. **5.** Activate your phone's camera. **6.** Hold the camera as if you were taking a picture of the QR code. **7.** The app will pick up the link to the web page. **8.** You should be online with Monkey Magic!

# What Can You Do?

• Want to make a difference? Contact an orangutan conservation organization to see how you can help.

• You may be able to "adopt" an orangutan (see back of this book for more information), raise money to support conservation, or write to people who can make a difference. Perhaps you could get your class or school to organize a petition.

• You can also tell your friends about orangutan conservation.

• And of course recommend *Monkey Magic – the Curse of Mukada*. For more ideas and information, check out the *Monkey Magic* website: www.monkeymagicbook.com and www.canofwormsenterprises.co.uk/monkeymagic

# Acknowledgements

The night was dark and creepy. We lay in our rickety wooden shack in the steamy rainforest, preparing to sleep on beds that creaked with every twitch and turn. Cicadas, birds and animals were in full cry.

"Daddy, please tell us a story! Please tell us a story!"

The request from my inspirations, Amy and Rosie, stalled an eagerly awaited sleep and prompted me to make up a tale about Robbie the proboscis monkey. That story would eventually evolve into *Monkey Magic*.

Like every dad, I am the luckiest dad.

My deepest gratitude goes to my wife and best friend, Linda, for her unbending support and selflessness of King Kong proportions. Without her promptings to go write for an hour here and there, I would not have reached this page.

An enormous "cheers" to Phil Tatham for guiding his publishing company into what for Monsoon Books is the uncharted jungle of children's fiction. Thanks also to Natalie Thompson for spotting the manuscript and to Evelyn S. Rogers for spotting the holes.

Many thanks to Raye Coates and her Canadian International School class in Singapore for giving Monkey Magic its first hearing. Heidi, Sara, Yoon, Kazuma, Amara, Te Jeong, Amy I., Caitlin, Jae Ho, Sakura, Andres, Isabella and Michael; your kind words meant so much, since the best judges of children's novels will always be children.

Every writer needs a writing buddy, and I was lucky to meet the journalist and author Vittoria D'Alessio. Thanks also to the many people who nudged my writing along in some way or another. They include Britney and Jessica Adam, Issy and Jade Clark, Pete Davies, Simon Grose-Hodge, Tony Grounds, the Laurence family, Violet Majendie, Sochi Mihori, Marie Nichols, Lisa Riley, Annabel Rutherford, Jo Sargent, Isobel Stoddart and Clarissa Tan. Thanks also to Andy Schuman for "tap-tap." And, of course, thanks to my parents.

Finally, my sincere gratitude goes to the kind folk who took time out of their busy schedules to read a novel by a complete stranger. Professor David Bellamy, Zac Goldsmith, Terri Irwin, Fanny Lai, Dr Christian Nellemann, Angela Royston and Jeremy Strong: good on you.

*This is a special preview of the next book in the series,*
**Monkey Magic 2: The Great Wall Mystery.**

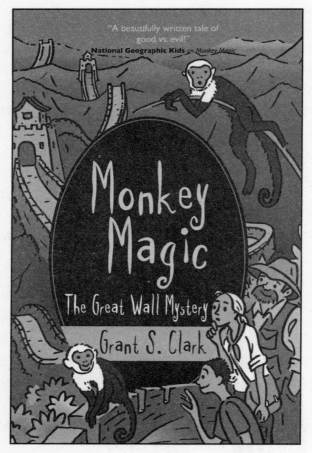

*Order your copy now from the publisher's website,*
**www.canofwormsenterprises.co.uk/monkeymagic**.

# Chapter 1

# TAP-TAP

Tap-tap on my shoulder. My eyelids are heavy, too heavy to open. Snug, sumptuous sleep smothers me like a cosy, warm blanket, begging me not to betray it for the waking world.

Another tap.

A memory stirs.

*Remember the orangutans*, a voice deep inside me pleads.

The anticipation kicks in. I can sense the fun, I can taste the adventure, I can feel the adrenalin. I am so ready for monkey magic. Desperate to see my ape friends after the horrors of the past week in Borneo, my eyes spring open to make out a blurry mass of fur.

"Sorry to wake you, hula girl."

Disappointment. This primate is no monkey.

"We've arrived," says Dad, lips hidden by bushy beard.

"Unless you want to stay in the car?"

Confusion. Three other faces stare at me from inside the car; a boy, a man, a woman, all Chinese. I am holding a stuffed monkey in a vehicle so plush the leather seats are as comfy as a sofa. Who are these people? Are we still in Borneo? Why doesn't Dad shave his beard off?

"It looks amazing," Dad says.

My fear that adults secretly read children's minds returns for an instant, but I realise he's not talking about the beard. Dad points outside and at last I remember. The three people met us at Beijing airport this morning after our overnight flight from Borneo. Dad is in China to speak at a conference and I have slept for most of the four-hour drive from Beijing.

The adults are from Shendang University; Professor Bo is running the conference, Dr Lim works with her and Pei is his nephew. The boy was reading a computer magazine when I dozed off gripping the monkey, a gift from the professor.

Trees, blue sky, some sort of castle or ruins rise higher than I can see through the car window. No, this most certainly is not Borneo. This is one of the wonders of the world.

"Wow," I say. "It's ... it's great."

"Actually, you are correct," says Pei. "The Great Wall of China."

And we are about to climb China's famous landmark to witness one of the most unusual invasions in its 2,000-year history; a gathering that will bring smiles to millions of people around the world but that will also lead to events that put my life in the gravest of danger.

\* \* \*

This wasn't one of the touristy sections of the Great Wall with cable cars or ski lifts. I had lost count at 300 steps and could taste sweat on my top lip.

"Nearly there," puffed Professor Bo. "It's worth the effort, my darlings."

The professor's gold-rimmed glasses, clunky handbag and diamond rings glistened in the sun. It was a clear, crisp day and we could see across the forest as far as the skyscrapers of Shendang.

"So we'll actually see them on the Great Wall?" asked Dad.

"Can," said Dr Lim, wearing a grey suit and tinted glasses with thick rims. I think by that he meant we could. He slid his fingers through greased-back dark hair.

"Thousands of people will come tomorrow so enjoy your sneak preview," said the professor.

"Why tomorrow?" I asked.

"Newspaper and television," said Dr Lim.

"The reporters will get their first look as soon as Dr Alexander – I mean your father – finishes his inspection," grinned the professor. "After the TV reports go out, the crowds will flock here."

I was intrigued how the professor never stopped smiling

and how her wavy black hair bounced like in shampoo ads.

She was the most cheerful and glamorous primatologist I'd ever met. Dr Lim was the complete opposite.

"Correct," he said in a deep, slow voice. "Like bears to honey."

Dad had only found out about this extra assignment when we were in Borneo this week. Shendang's mayor had demanded a report from a foreign expert on the strange sightings at the Great Wall that began a few days ago. Dad, already coming to speak at the conference, was the obvious choice. Professor Bo had already submitted a report on behalf of the zoology department. Dr Jeremy Alexander had until tomorrow to provide his.

We climbed the final steps to the top of the grey stone wall and joined a cobbled track stretching in both directions to the horizon. Lined with turrets, the Great Wall snaked gracefully between mountain peaks, rising and falling like a roller coaster through the clouds.

"It's stunning!" I said, breeze blowing hair in my eyes.

"That is a logical reaction," said Dr Lim's nephew.

Pei was about my age and, like me, was dressed in jeans and a T-shirt. My shirt read: "Save the Planet: It's the only one with orangutans and chocolate." His had a picture of a laptop. Pei lived in Beijing and, I suspect, had been dragged along to the conference to keep me company. Dad had warned me we were the only kids coming.

"I will never tire of this view, darlings," said the professor.

"But we must press on before the reporters arrive."

The Great Wall was split into sections divided by stone shelters, like mini castles with arched windows. Shendang came in and out of view as clouds rolled by.

"There's the university," said Professor Bo, pointing to a red-brick building halfway to the city. "See our magnificent panda fountain?"

I was only tall enough to see the fountain's jet of water shooting skyward. Something on the path ahead caught my attention: a man was taking pictures at the highest point of the wall outside one of the mini castles.

"Looks like the photographers got there before us," said the professor.

The next stretch was the steepest and I tried to ignore the aching in my legs. Professor Bo greeted the cameraman in Mandarin. He said nothing and kept snapping photos, his expression surly, his black raincoat flapping in the breeze. A cigarette hung from his mouth and another dangled between two fingers of a hand that clasped a long-lens camera.

Strangely, neither of the cigarettes were lit. He was within touching distance of us but still took another photograph, the lens almost brushing Dad's nose, then hobbled by, gripping the wall like a man twice his age.

"Some people have no manners," said Professor Bo.

"What kind of journalist doesn't ask questions?" Dad wondered.

"I guess he got the pictures he wanted and before anyone

else," the professor said. "We'd better hurry too or the reporters will catch up. It's just over the crest, my dears, if you lead the way, doctor."

"Can," Dr Lim replied.

We entered the highest shelter as a cloud arrived. Finally, the mist cleared to reveal the reason why we had trekked to this remote part of the 6,400-kilometre wall.

It was no disappointment.

We hope you enjoyed this special preview of the next book in the series, **Monkey Magic 2: The Great Wall Mystery.**

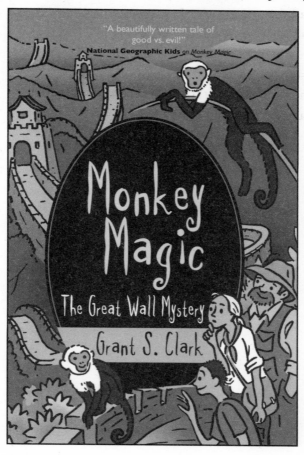

Order your copy now from the publisher's website,
**www.canofwormsenterprises.co.uk/monkeymagic**.

## About the Publisher

The Monkey Magic series is published by Can of Worms Kids Press, part of a wriggling writhing collective of book publishers run by Can of Worms Enterprises Ltd.

In addition to the Monkey Magic series, Can of Worms Kids Press also publishes the Boing-Boing, The Boy Who Biked the World and Mission:Explore series.

We also do wonderful comic versions of Shakespeare's plays illustrated by more fantastic people.
www.graphicshakespeare.com

And for those kids who have grown up or are aspiring to, we have stories about ordinary people doing extraordinary things: climbing mountains, finding cannibals, trekking to the North or South Pole, cycling around the world and many other amazing adventures, all published by Eye Books.

You can find out about all of our books and get special offers at www.canofwormsenterprises.co.uk

# MISSION:EXPLORE

"Bold, cool, exciting and just plain fun!"
National Geographic

The **Mission:Explore** books challenge girls and boys in daring new ways. Encouraging children to draw, rub, smear, write, scrape and print their findings & achievements as they complete each mission, the books promote interaction with and exploration of the world around them.

See opposite for an example mission to try!

978-1-904872-33-7
£5.99

978-1-904872-38-2
£4.99

978-1-904872-41-2
£4.99

"Designed to be read, scribbled on, illustrated, smeared, scratched and sniffed, it may just be the most revolutionary geography-related book ever published."

Geographical Magazine

# www.missionexplore.co.uk

## ☐ MEC016
# Be quiet

Sit silently in nature for
30 minutes. What do you see?

Keep notes.

## ☐ MET001
# Dice-nav

Assign an action to each number on a set of dice. Go on
a journey and follow the dice commands.

Where do you end up?

## The Boy Who Biked the World
### On the Road to Africa

Alastair Humphreys
Illustrations by Tom Morgan-Jones
978-1-903070-75-8

In this charming caricature of Alastair Humphreys' infamous circumnavigation of the world on his bike, children are swept along with the character of Tom, an adventurous boy who feels there must be more to life than school!

The first part of *The Boy Who Biked the World* follows Tom leaving England, cycling through Europe and all the way through Africa to the tip of South Africa. Along the way, young readers are introduced not only to the various fascinating landmarks and landscapes he passes through, but also to the various people who so happily embraced him as he travelled on his journey.

With engaging illustrations, postcards and journal entries throughout, this book provides an immersive experience for any young adventurer!

**Alastair Humphreys** spent four years cycling round the world, a journey of 46,000 miles across five continents. His adventure is told in two books: *Moods of Future Joys* and *Thunder & Sunshine*.

# Boing-Boing the bionic cat

"Boing-Boing is a small furry feline who has saved the Natural History Museum from a jewel thief, an Egyptologist from the Mummy's Revenge … and has made thousands of children laugh – Boing-Boing, bionic cat and superhero."

*Evening Standard*

Daniel, who loves cats but is allergic to them, is delighted when his neighbour Professor George, an engineer, builds him a bionic cat. The Boing-Boing series tells of the adventures they have together, using real scientific concepts and existing technologies. Boing-Boing is science fact not science fiction.

Boing-Boing the Bionic Cat
… and the Space Station
Illustrations by Tom Morgan-Jones
ISBN: 978-1-904872-07-8

A massive solar flare is heading towards the International Space Station, endangering all the astronauts on board. With the clock ticking, Boing-Boing and Daniel are the only ones capable of moving the Space Station to safety.

Will the new design features protect Boing-Boing against the dangers of outer space? Will the solar flare engulf all in its path or can Boing-Boing save the day and return unharmed to Earth?

# WOULD YOU LIKE TO ADOPT AN ORANGUTAN?

### *www.savetheorangutan.org.uk*

*Help care for these playful, curious & beautiful creatures, and help us make sure that there'll always be orangutans in the rainforests.*

Miko               Nika               Hercules

Because Hercules isn't cute and cuddly, not many people want to adopt him. This is sad, because he's a beautiful and gentle orangutan who had a very sad life before he was taken to Nyaru Menteng. He lived in a tiny cage for many years, and his hands and feet were crippled. He'll never again be able to climb trees, so he can't be set free to live in the wild. By adopting Hercules you could make sure that he has a happy life on his island.

Miko arrived at Nyaru Menteng when he was really tiny. He had been kept in a village in Borneo as a pet, but had not been well cared for – one of his little hands and some of his fingers had been hurt. Miko is a sweet little chap who is now 3 years old, and goes to Forest School every day to learn all about life in the rainforest. He loves playing in the trees and having fun with his friends.

When Nita was a baby, she was taken from her mother and kept as a pet. Her owners did their best for her, but orangutans are wild animals and need to live in the forest. Nita was very thin when she arrived at Nyaru Menteng, because she had never been given orangutan food. She now eats fresh leaves and fruit from the forest so that she'll grow strong and healthy. She's very shy and is still learning how to climb trees, but soon she'll be playing in the forest with her little orangutan friends.

If you'd like to adopt Hercules, Miko or Nita, please turn the page.

# Orangutans are a very important part of our world.

On an island called Borneo, in Indonesia, orangutans swing from branch to branch in the rainforests using their long arms and strong toes. They eat fruit from the forests & make nests high in the trees each night.

Sadly, people are cutting down the forests to plant oil palm trees.

People sell fruit from these trees to make chocolate, crisps & soap. Things they could use instead cost more than palm oil. When the rainforests are cut down, orangutans have nowhere to live. Without our help, there will be no more orangutans left in the wild.

In Borneo, special rescue centres exist for homeless orangutans. Some are babies whose mothers have died, and they need to be cared for until they're older. One of the centres is called Nyaru Menteng, where ladies called "babysitters" take care of the young orangutans. Each day, they take them into the forest where they learn what food to eat, how to build nests, what dangers are in the forest and learn how to climb and swing from tree to tree. Mostly, though, they laugh and play until it's time to go home.

When they return to Nyaru Menteng in the afternoon, they play on jungle-gyms, swings and ropes until it's time for bed. They sleep in a nursery full of laundry baskets in which the babysitters make them beds.

When they are 10 years old, they will move to an island in the nearby river where they'll be given food and be carefully watched to make sure that they're happy away from the safety of Nyaru Menteng. A few years after that they'll be taken to a safe rainforest and set free to live in the wild.

If you'd like to adopt Hercules, Miko or Nita, *or any of our other orangutans, go to our website:* ***www.savetheorangutan.org.uk*** *or call on **08456 521 528**. Outside the UK, call **+44 20 7531 1042**.*